This Feelings Journal Belongs To:

Claire

My Feelings Journal © 2019 by Matilda Boyd

Date: **2020**

Today I feel **Happy**.

This is a picture of how I'm feeling today ...

I feel this way because ...

I got this book.

Something that might help me feel better is ...

_____

_____

_____

_____

_____

_____

Picture of me doing this ...

Someone who I would like to share my
feelings with is **Mommy**.
I will do this by (talking) to them / writing
them a note. (Circle one)

Dear _____,

Today I feel _____

because _____

_____

_____

_____

_____

_____

_____

_____

_____

_____

_____

_____

_____

*The back of this page is left blank so that you can draw a picture of how you feel and tear this page out of your journal to give someone your message.

Date: _____

Today I feel _____.

😊 😍 😜 😟 😢 😬 😠

This is a picture of how I'm feeling today ...

I feel this way because ...

_____

_____

_____

_____

_____

_____

_____

Something that might help me feel better is ...

_____

_____

_____

_____

_____

_____

Picture of me doing this ...

Someone who I would like to share my

feelings with is _____.

I will do this by talking to them / writing

them a note. (Circle one)

Dear _____,

Today I feel _____

because _____

_____

_____

_____

_____

_____

_____

_____

_____

_____

_____

_____

_____

*The back of this page is left blank so that you can draw a picture of
how you feel and tear this page out of your journal to give someone
your message.

Date: _____

Today I feel _____.

😊 😍 😜 😞 😢 😬 😠

This is a picture of how I'm feeling today ...

I feel this way because ...

_____

_____

_____

_____

_____

_____

_____

Something that might help me feel better is ...

_____

_____

_____

_____

_____

_____

Picture of me doing this ...

Someone who I would like to share my

feelings with is _____.

I will do this by talking to them / writing

them a note. (Circle one)

Dear _____,

Today I feel _____

because _____

_____

_____

_____

_____

_____

_____

_____

_____

_____

_____

_____

*The back of this page is left blank so that you can draw a picture of how you feel and tear this page out of your journal to give someone your message.

Date: _____

Today I feel _____.

This is a picture of how I'm feeling today ...

I feel this way because ...

_____

_____

_____

_____

_____

_____

_____

Something that might help me feel better is ...

_____

_____

_____

_____

_____

_____

Picture of me doing this ...

Someone who I would like to share my

feelings with is _____.

I will do this by talking to them / writing

them a note. (Circle one)

Dear _____,

Today I feel _____

because _____

_____

_____

_____

_____

_____

_____

_____

_____

_____

_____

_____

_____

*The back of this page is left blank so that you can draw a picture of how you feel and tear this page out of your journal to give someone your message.

Date: _____

Today I feel _____.

This is a picture of how I'm feeling today ...

I feel this way because ...

_____

_____

_____

_____

_____

_____

_____

Something that might help me feel better is ...

_____

_____

_____

_____

_____

_____

Picture of me doing this ...

Someone who I would like to share my

feelings with is _____.

I will do this by talking to them / writing

them a note. (Circle one)

Dear _____,

Today I feel _____

because _____

_____

_____

_____

_____

_____

_____

_____

_____

_____

_____

_____

_____

*The back of this page is left blank so that you can draw a picture of how you feel and tear this page out of your journal to give someone your message.

Date: _____

Today I feel _____.

This is a picture of how I'm feeling today ...

I feel this way because ...

_____

_____

_____

_____

_____

_____

Something that might help me feel better is ...

_____

_____

_____

_____

_____

_____

Picture of me doing this ...

Someone who I would like to share my

feelings with is _____.

I will do this by talking to them / writing

them a note. (Circle one)

Dear _____,

Today I feel _____

because _____

_____

_____

_____

_____

_____

_____

_____

_____

_____

_____

_____

_____

*The back of this page is left blank so that you can draw a picture of how you feel and tear this page out of your journal to give someone your message.

Date: _____

Today I feel _____.

This is a picture of how I'm feeling today ...

I feel this way because ...

_____

_____

_____

_____

_____

_____

_____

Something that might help me feel better is ...

_____

_____

_____

_____

_____

_____

Picture of me doing this ...

Someone who I would like to share my

feelings with is _____.

I will do this by talking to them / writing

them a note. (Circle one)

Dear _____,

Today I feel _____

because _____

_____

_____

_____

_____

_____

_____

_____

_____

_____

_____

_____

_____

*The back of this page is left blank so that you can draw a picture of how you feel and tear this page out of your journal to give someone your message.

Date: _____

Today I feel _____.

This is a picture of how I'm feeling today ...

I feel this way because ...

_____

_____

_____

_____

_____

_____

_____

Something that might help me feel better is ...

_____

_____

_____

_____

_____

_____

Picture of me doing this ...

Someone who I would like to share my

feelings with is _____.

I will do this by talking to them / writing

them a note. (Circle one)

Dear _____,

Today I feel _____

because _____

_____

_____

_____

_____

_____

_____

_____

_____

_____

_____

_____

_____

*The back of this page is left blank so that you can draw a picture of how you feel and tear this page out of your journal to give someone your message.

Date: _____

Today I feel _____.

😊 😍 😜 😟 😢 😬 😠

This is a picture of how I'm feeling today ...

I feel this way because ...

_____

_____

_____

_____

_____

_____

_____

Something that might help me feel better is ...

_____

_____

_____

_____

_____

_____

Picture of me doing this ...

Someone who I would like to share my

feelings with is _____.

I will do this by talking to them / writing

them a note. (Circle one)

Dear _____,

Today I feel _____

because _____

_____

_____

_____

_____

_____

_____

_____

_____

_____

_____

_____

*The back of this page is left blank so that you can draw a picture of how you feel and tear this page out of your journal to give someone your message.

Date: _____

Today I feel _____.

This is a picture of how I'm feeling today ...

I feel this way because ...

_____

_____

_____

_____

_____

_____

_____

Something that might help me feel better is ...

_____

_____

_____

_____

_____

_____

Picture of me doing this ...

Someone who I would like to share my

feelings with is _____.

I will do this by talking to them / writing

them a note. (Circle one)

Dear _____,

Today I feel _____

because _____

_____

_____

_____

_____

_____

_____

_____

_____

_____

_____

_____

_____

*The back of this page is left blank so that you can draw a picture of how you feel and tear this page out of your journal to give someone your message.

Date: _____

Today I feel _____.

This is a picture of how I'm feeling today ...

I feel this way because ...

_____

_____

_____

_____

_____

_____

_____

Something that might help me feel better is ...

_____

_____

_____

_____

_____

_____

Picture of me doing this ...

Someone who I would like to share my

feelings with is _____.

I will do this by talking to them / writing

them a note. (Circle one)

Dear _____,

Today I feel _____

because _____

_____

_____

_____

_____

_____

_____

_____

_____

_____

_____

_____

_____

*The back of this page is left blank so that you can draw a picture of how you feel and tear this page out of your journal to give someone your message.

Date: _____

Today I feel _____.

This is a picture of how I'm feeling today ...

I feel this way because ...

_____

_____

_____

_____

_____

_____

_____

Something that might help me feel better is ...

_____

_____

_____

_____

_____

_____

Picture of me doing this ...

Someone who I would like to share my

feelings with is _____.

I will do this by talking to them / writing

them a note. (Circle one)

Dear _____,

Today I feel _____

because _____

_____

_____

_____

_____

_____

_____

_____

_____

_____

_____

_____

_____

_____

*The back of this page is left blank so that you can draw a picture of
how you feel and tear this page out of your journal to give someone
your message.

Date: _____

Today I feel _____.

This is a picture of how I'm feeling today ...

I feel this way because ...

_____

_____

_____

_____

_____

_____

_____

Something that might help me feel better is ...

_____

_____

_____

_____

_____

_____

Picture of me doing this ...

Someone who I would like to share my

feelings with is _____.

I will do this by talking to them / writing

them a note. (Circle one)

Dear _____,

Today I feel _____

because _____

_____

_____

_____

_____

_____

_____

_____

_____

_____

_____

_____

_____

*The back of this page is left blank so that you can draw a picture of how you feel and tear this page out of your journal to give someone your message.

Date: _____

Today I feel _____.

This is a picture of how I'm feeling today ...

I feel this way because ...

_____

_____

_____

_____

_____

_____

Something that might help me feel better is ...

_____

_____

_____

_____

_____

Picture of me doing this ...

Someone who I would like to share my

feelings with is _____.

I will do this by talking to them / writing

them a note. (Circle one)

Dear _____,

Today I feel _____

because _____

_____

_____

_____

_____

_____

_____

_____

_____

_____

_____

_____

_____

*The back of this page is left blank so that you can draw a picture of
how you feel and tear this page out of your journal to give someone
your message.

Date: _____

Today I feel _____.

😊 😍 😜 😟 😢 😬 😠

This is a picture of how I'm feeling today ...

I feel this way because ...

_____

_____

_____

_____

_____

_____

Something that might help me feel better is ...

_____

_____

_____

_____

_____

_____

Picture of me doing this ...

Someone who I would like to share my

feelings with is _____.

I will do this by talking to them / writing

them a note. (Circle one)

Dear _____,

Today I feel _____

because _____

_____

_____

_____

_____

_____

_____

_____

_____

_____

_____

_____

_____

*The back of this page is left blank so that you can draw a picture of how you feel and tear this page out of your journal to give someone your message.

Date: _____

Today I feel _____.

😊 😍 😜 😟 😢 😬 😠

This is a picture of how I'm feeling today ...

I feel this way because ...

_____

_____

_____

_____

_____

_____

_____

Something that might help me feel better is ...

_____

_____

_____

_____

_____

Picture of me doing this ...

Someone who I would like to share my

feelings with is _____.

I will do this by talking to them / writing

them a note. (Circle one)

Dear _____,

Today I feel _____

because _____

_____

_____

_____

_____

_____

_____

_____

_____

_____

_____

_____

*The back of this page is left blank so that you can draw a picture of
how you feel and tear this page out of your journal to give someone
your message.

Date: _____

Today I feel _____.

This is a picture of how I'm feeling today ...

I feel this way because ...

_____

_____

_____

_____

_____

_____

Something that might help me feel better is ...

_____

_____

_____

_____

_____

_____

Picture of me doing this ...

Someone who I would like to share my

feelings with is _____.

I will do this by talking to them / writing

them a note. (Circle one)

Dear _____,

Today I feel _____

because _____

_____

_____

_____

_____

_____

_____

_____

_____

_____

_____

_____

*The back of this page is left blank so that you can draw a picture of how you feel and tear this page out of your journal to give someone your message.

Date: _____

Today I feel _____.

😊 😍 😜 😟 😢 😬 😠

This is a picture of how I'm feeling today ...

I feel this way because ...

_____

_____

_____

_____

_____

_____

Something that might help me feel better is ...

_____

_____

_____

_____

_____

_____

Picture of me doing this ...

Someone who I would like to share my

feelings with is _____.

I will do this by talking to them / writing

them a note. (Circle one)

Dear _____,

Today I feel _____

because _____

_____

_____

_____

_____

_____

_____

_____

_____

_____

_____

_____

*The back of this page is left blank so that you can draw a picture of how you feel and tear this page out of your journal to give someone your message.

Date: _____

Today I feel _____.

😊 😍 😜 😟 😢 😬 😠

This is a picture of how I'm feeling today ...

I feel this way because ...

_____

_____

_____

_____

_____

_____

_____

Something that might help me feel better is ...

_____

_____

_____

_____

_____

_____

Picture of me doing this ...

Someone who I would like to share my

feelings with is _____.

I will do this by talking to them / writing

them a note. (Circle one)

Dear _____,

Today I feel _____

because _____

_____

_____

_____

_____

_____

_____

_____

_____

_____

_____

_____

*The back of this page is left blank so that you can draw a picture of how you feel and tear this page out of your journal to give someone your message.

Date: _____

Today I feel _____.

This is a picture of how I'm feeling today ...

I feel this way because ...

_____

_____

_____

_____

_____

_____

_____

Something that might help me feel better is ...

_____

_____

_____

_____

_____

_____

Picture of me doing this ...

Someone who I would like to share my

feelings with is _____ .

I will do this by talking to them / writing

them a note. (Circle one)

Dear _____ ,

Today I feel _____

because _____

_____

_____

_____

_____

_____

_____

_____

_____

_____

_____

_____

*The back of this page is left blank so that you can draw a picture of
how you feel and tear this page out of your journal to give someone
your message.

Date: _____

Today I feel _____.

😊 😍 😜 😟 😢 😬 😠

This is a picture of how I'm feeling today ...

I feel this way because ...

_____

_____

_____

_____

_____

_____

_____

Something that might help me feel better is ...

_____

_____

_____

_____

_____

_____

Picture of me doing this ...

Someone who I would like to share my

feelings with is _____.

I will do this by talking to them / writing

them a note. (Circle one)

Dear _____,

Today I feel _____

because _____

_____

_____

_____

_____

_____

_____

_____

_____

_____

_____

_____

_____

*The back of this page is left blank so that you can draw a picture of how you feel and tear this page out of your journal to give someone your message.

Date: _____

Today I feel _____.

This is a picture of how I'm feeling today ...

I feel this way because ...

_____
_____
_____
_____
_____
_____
_____

Something that might help me feel better is ...

_____

_____

_____

_____

_____

_____

Picture of me doing this ...

Someone who I would like to share my

feelings with is _____.

I will do this by talking to them / writing

them a note. (Circle one)

Dear _____,

Today I feel _____

because _____

_____

_____

_____

_____

_____

_____

_____

_____

_____

_____

_____

*The back of this page is left blank so that you can draw a picture of
how you feel and tear this page out of your journal to give someone
your message.

Date: _____

Today I feel _____.

This is a picture of how I'm feeling today ...

I feel this way because ...

_____

_____

_____

_____

_____

_____

_____

Something that might help me feel better is ...

_____

_____

_____

_____

_____

_____

Picture of me doing this ...

Someone who I would like to share my

feelings with is _____.

I will do this by talking to them / writing

them a note. (Circle one)

Dear _____,

Today I feel _____

because _____

_____

_____

_____

_____

_____

_____

_____

_____

_____

_____

*The back of this page is left blank so that you can draw a picture of
how you feel and tear this page out of your journal to give someone
your message.

Date: _____

Today I feel _____.

This is a picture of how I'm feeling today ...

I feel this way because ...

_____

_____

_____

_____

_____

_____

_____

Something that might help me feel better is ...

_____

_____

_____

_____

_____

_____

Picture of me doing this ...

Someone who I would like to share my

feelings with is _____.

I will do this by talking to them / writing

them a note. (Circle one)

Dear _____,

Today I feel _____

because _____

_____

_____

_____

_____

_____

_____

_____

_____

_____

_____

_____

*The back of this page is left blank so that you can draw a picture of how you feel and tear this page out of your journal to give someone your message.

Date: _____

Today I feel _____.

This is a picture of how I'm feeling today ...

I feel this way because ...

_____

_____

_____

_____

_____

_____

_____

Something that might help me feel better is ...

_____

_____

_____

_____

_____

Picture of me doing this ...

Someone who I would like to share my

feelings with is _____.

I will do this by talking to them / writing

them a note. (Circle one)

Dear _____,

Today I feel _____

because _____

_____

_____

_____

_____

_____

_____

_____

_____

_____

_____

_____

_____

*The back of this page is left blank so that you can draw a picture of
how you feel and tear this page out of your journal to give someone
your message.

Date: _____

Today I feel _____.

This is a picture of how I'm feeling today ...

I feel this way because ...

_____

_____

_____

_____

_____

_____

_____

Something that might help me feel better is ...

_____

_____

_____

_____

_____

_____

Picture of me doing this ...

Someone who I would like to share my

feelings with is _____ .

I will do this by talking to them / writing

them a note. (Circle one)

Dear _____,

Today I feel _____

because _____

_____

_____

_____

_____

_____

_____

_____

_____

_____

_____

_____

_____

*The back of this page is left blank so that you can draw a picture of
how you feel and tear this page out of your journal to give someone
your message.

Date: _____

Today I feel _____.

This is a picture of how I'm feeling today ...

I feel this way because ...

_____

_____

_____

_____

_____

_____

Something that might help me feel better is ...

_____

_____

_____

_____

_____

_____

Picture of me doing this ...

Someone who I would like to share my

feelings with is _____.

I will do this by talking to them / writing

them a note. (Circle one)

Dear _____,

Today I feel _____

because _____

_____

_____

_____

_____

_____

_____

_____

_____

_____

_____

_____

*The back of this page is left blank so that you can draw a picture of
how you feel and tear this page out of your journal to give someone
your message.

Date: _____

Today I feel _____.

😊 😍 😜 😟 😢 😬 😠

This is a picture of how I'm feeling today ...

I feel this way because ...

_____

_____

_____

_____

_____

_____

_____

Something that might help me feel better is ...

_____

_____

_____

_____

_____

_____

Picture of me doing this ...

Someone who I would like to share my

feelings with is _____.

I will do this by talking to them / writing

them a note. (Circle one)

Dear _____,

Today I feel _____

because _____

_____

_____

_____

_____

_____

_____

_____

_____

_____

_____

_____

_____

*The back of this page is left blank so that you can draw a picture of
how you feel and tear this page out of your journal to give someone
your message.

Date: _____

Today I feel _____.

This is a picture of how I'm feeling today ...

I feel this way because ...

_____

_____

_____

_____

_____

_____

Something that might help me feel better is ...

_____

_____

_____

_____

_____

_____

Picture of me doing this ...

Someone who I would like to share my

feelings with is _____.

I will do this by talking to them / writing

them a note. (Circle one)

Dear _____,

Today I feel _____

because _____

_____

_____

_____

_____

_____

_____

_____

_____

_____

_____

_____

_____

*The back of this page is left blank so that you can draw a picture of
how you feel and tear this page out of your journal to give someone
your message.

Date: _____

Today I feel _____.

😊 😍 😜 😟 😢 😬 😠

This is a picture of how I'm feeling today ...

I feel this way because ...

_____

_____

_____

_____

_____

_____

_____

Something that might help me feel better is ...

_____

_____

_____

_____

_____

Picture of me doing this ...

Someone who I would like to share my

feelings with is _____.

I will do this by talking to them / writing

them a note. (Circle one)

Dear _____,

Today I feel _____

because _____

_____

_____

_____

_____

_____

_____

_____

_____

_____

_____

_____

_____

*The back of this page is left blank so that you can draw a picture of how you feel and tear this page out of your journal to give someone your message.

Made in the USA
Columbia, SC
27 February 2020

88475713R00067